1935 if you wanted to
read a good book, you needed
either a lot of money or a library card.
Cheap paperbacks were available, but their
poor production generally mirrored the quality
between the covers. One weekend that year,
Allen Lane, Managing Director of The Bodley Head,
having spent the weekend visiting Agatha Christie,
found himself on a platform at Exeter station trying to
find something to read for his journey back to London.
He was appalled by the quality of the material he had to
choose from. Everything that Allen Lane achieved from that
day until his death in 1970 was based on a passionate belief
in the existence of 'a vast reading public for *intelligent*
books at a low price'. The result of his momentous vision
was the birth not only of Penguin, but of the 'paperback
revolution'. Quality writing became available for the price of
a packet of cigarettes, literature became a mass medium
for the first time, a nation of book-borrowers became a
nation of book-buyers – and the very concept of book
publishing was changed for ever. Those founding
principles – of quality and value, with an overarching
belief in the fundamental importance of reading –
have guided everything the company has
done since 1935. Sir Allen Lane's
pioneering spirit is still very much alive
at Penguin in 2005. Here's to
the next 70 years!

MORE THAN A BUSINESS

'We decided it was time to end the almost customary half-hearted manner in which cheap editions were produced – as though the only people who could possibly want cheap editions must belong to a lower order of intelligence. We, however, believed in the existence in this country of a vast reading public for intelligent books at a low price, and staked everything on it'
Sir Allen Lane, 1902–1970

'The Penguin Books are splendid value for sixpence, so splendid that if other publishers had any sense they would combine against them and suppress them'
George Orwell

'More than a business … a national cultural asset'
Guardian

'When you look at the whole Penguin achievement you know that it constitutes, in action, one of the more democratic successes of our recent social history'
Richard Hoggart

Cloud, Castle, Lake

VLADIMIR NABOKOV

PENGUIN BOOKS

PENGUIN BOOKS

Published by the Penguin Group
Penguin Books Ltd, 80 Strand, London WC2R ORL, England
Penguin Group (USA) Inc., 375 Hudson Street, New York, New York 10014, USA
Penguin Group (Canada), 10 Alcorn Avenue, Toronto, Ontario, Canada M4V 3B2
(a division of Pearson Penguin Canada Inc.)
Penguin Ireland, 25 St Stephen's Green, Dublin 2, Ireland
(a division of Penguin Books Ltd)
Penguin Group (Australia), 250 Camberwell Road, Camberwell, Victoria 3124,
Australia (a division of Pearson Australia Group Pty Ltd)
Penguin Books India Pvt Ltd, 11 Community Centre,
Panchsheel Park, New Delhi – 110 017, India
Penguin Group (NZ), cnr Airborne and Rosedale Roads, Albany,
Auckland 1310, New Zealand (a division of Pearson New Zealand Ltd)
Penguin Books (South Africa) (Pty) Ltd, 24 Sturdee Avenue,
Rosebank 2196, South Africa

Penguin Books Ltd, Registered Offices: 80 Strand, London WC2R ORL, England

www.penguin.com

First published in *The Stories of Vladimir Nabokov*
in the USA by Alfred A. Knopf 1995
First published in Great Britain by Weidenfeld & Nicolson 1996
Published in Penguin Books as *Collected Stories* 1997
This selection published as a Pocket Penguin 2005

1

Copyright © Dmitri Nabokov, 1995
All rights reserved

Set in 11.5/13.5pt Monotype Dante
Typeset by Palimpsest Book Production Limited
Polmont, Stirlingshire
Printed in England by Clays Ltd, St Ives plc

Contents

The Admiralty Spire

You will please pardon me, dear Madam, but I am a rude and straightforward person, so I'll come right out with it: do not labor under any delusion: this is far from being a fan letter. On the contrary, as you will realize yourself in a minute, it is a rather odd little epistle that, who knows, might serve as a lesson of sorts not only for you but for other impetuous lady novelists as well. I hasten, first of all, to introduce myself, so that my visual image may show through like a watermark; this is much more honest than to encourage by silence the incorrect conclusions that the eye involuntarily draws from the calligraphy of penned lines. No, in spite of my slender handwriting and the youthful flourish of my commas, I am stout and middle-aged; true, my corpulence is not flabby, but has piquancy, zest, waspishness. It is far removed, Madam, from the turndown collars of the poet Apukhtin, the fat pet of ladies. But that will do. You, as a writer, have already collected these clues to fill in the rest of me. *Bonjour, Madame.* And now let's get down to business.

The other day at a Russian library, relegated by illiterate fate to a murky Berlin alleyway, I took out three or four new items, and among them your novel *The Admiralty Spire*. Neat title – if for no other reason than that it is, isn't it, an iambic tetrameter, *admiraltéyskaya iglá,* and a famous Pushkinian line to boot. But it was the very neatness of that title that boded no good. Besides, I am generally wary of books published in the backwoods of our expatriation, such as Riga or Reval. Nevertheless, as I was saying, I did take your novel.

Ah, my dear Madam, ah, 'Mr.' Serge Solntsev, how easy it is to guess that the author's name is a pseudonym, that the author is not a man! Every sentence of yours buttons to the left. Your predilection for such expressions as 'time passed' or 'cuddled up *frileusement* in Mother's shawl,' the inevitable appearance of an episodic ensign (straight from imitations of *War and Peace*) who pronounces the letter *r* as a hard *g*, and, finally, footnotes with translations of French clichés, afford sufficient indication of your literary skill. But all this is only half the trouble.

Imagine the following: suppose I once took a walk through a marvelous landscape, where turbulent waters tumble and bindweed chokes the columns of desolate ruins, and then, many years later, in a stranger's house, I come across a snapshot showing me in a swaggering pose in front of what is obviously a pasteboard pillar; in the background there is the whitish smear of a daubed-in cascade, and somebody has inked a mustache on me. Where did the thing come from? Take away this horror! The dinning waters I remember were real, and, what is more, no one took a picture of me there.

Shall I interpret the parable for you? Shall I tell you that I had the same feeling, only nastier and sillier, on reading your nimble handiwork, your terrible *Spire*? As my index finger burst the uncut pages open and my eyes raced along the lines, I could only blink from the bewildering shock.

Do you wish to know what happened? Glad to oblige. As you lay massively in your hammock and recklessly allowed your pen to flow like a fountain (a near pun), you, Madam, wrote the story of my first love. Yes, a bewildering shock, and, as I too am a massive person, bewilderment is accompanied by shortness of breath. By now you and I are both puffing, for, doubtless, you are also dumbfounded by the sudden appearance of the hero that you invented. No, that was a slip – the trimmings are yours, I'll concede, and so are the stuffing and the sauce, but the game (another near pun), the game, Madam, is not yours but mine, with my buckshot in its wing. I am amazed – where and how could a lady unknown to me have kidnapped my past? Must I admit the possibility that you are acquainted with Katya – that you are close friends, even – and that she blabbed the whole business, as she whiled away summer crepuscles under the Baltic pines with you, the voracious novelist? But how did you dare, where did you find the gall not only to use Katya's tale, but, on top of that, to distort it so irreparably?

Since the day of our last meeting there has been a lapse of sixteen years – the age of a bride, an old dog, or the Soviet republic. Incidentally, let us note the first, but not the worst by far, of your innumerable and sloppy mistakes: Katya and I are not coevals. I was going on eighteen, and she on twenty. Relying on a tried and true method, you have your heroine strip before a full-length mirror whereupon you proceed to describe her loose hair, ash-blond of course, and her young curves. According to you her cornflower eyes would turn violet in pensive moments – a botanical miracle! You shaded them with the black fringe of lashes which, if I may make a contribution of my own, seemed longer toward the outer corners, giving her eyes a very special, though illusory, slant. Katya's figure was graceful, but she cultivated a slight stoop, and would lift her shoulders as she entered a room. You make her a stately maiden with contralto tones in her voice.

Sheer torture. I had a mind to copy out your images, all of which ring false, and scathingly juxtapose my infallible observations, but the result would have been 'nightmarish nonsense,' as the real Katya would have said, for the Logos allotted me does not possess sufficient precision or power to get disentangled from you. On the contrary, I myself get bogged down in the sticky snares of your conventional descriptions, and have no strength left to liberate Katya from your pen. Nevertheless, like Hamlet, I will argue, and, in the end, will out-argue you.

The theme of your concoction is love: a slightly decadent love with the February Revolution for backdrop, but still, love. Katya has been renamed Olga by you, and I have become Leonid. Well and good. Our first encounter, at the house of friends on Christmas Eve; our meetings at the Yusupov Skating Rink; her room, its indigo wallpaper, its mahogany furniture, and its only ornament, a porcelain ballerina with lifted leg – this is all right, this is all true. Except that you managed to give it all a taint of pretentious fabrication. As he takes his seat at the Parisiana Cinema on Nevsky Avenue, Leonid, a student of the Imperial Lyceum, puts his gloves in his three-cornered hat, while a couple of pages later he is already wearing civilian clothes: he doffs his bowler, and the reader is faced by an elegant young man, with his hair parted *à l'anglaise* exactly in the middle of his small, lacquered-looking head, and a purple handkerchief drooping out of his breast pocket. I do in fact remember dressing like the film actor Max Linder, and recall the generous spurts of *Vezhetal* lotion cooling my scalp, and Monsieur Pierre taking aim with his comb and flipping my hair over with a linotype swing, and then, as he yanked

off the sheet, yelling to a middle-aged, musta-
chioed fellow, 'Boy! Bross off the 'air!' Today my
memory reacts with irony to the breast-pocket
handkerchief and white spats of those days, but,
on the other hand, can in no way reconcile the
remembered torments of adolescent shaving with
your Leonid's 'smooth opaque pallor.' And I shall
leave on your conscience his Lermontovian lusterless eyes and aristocratic profile, as it is impossible
to discern much today because of an unexpected
increase in fleshiness.

Good Lord, keep me from bogging down in the
prose of this lady writer, whom I do not know
and do not wish to know, but who has encroached
with astonishing insolence on another person's
past! How dare you write, 'The pretty Christmas
tree with its *chatoyant* lights seemed to augur to
them joy jubilant'? You have extinguished the
whole tree with your breath, for one adjective
placed after the noun for the sake of elegance is
enough to kill the best of recollections. Before the
disaster, i.e., before your book, one such recollec-
tion of mine was the rippling, fragmentary light
in Katya's eyes, and the cherry reflection on her
cheek from the glossy little dollhouse of plasmic
paper hanging on a branch as, brushing aside the
bristly foliage, she stretched to pinch out the flame
of a candle that had gone berserk. What do I have
left of all this? Nothing – just a nauseating whiff
of literary combustion.

Your version gives the impression that Katya and I inhabited a kind of exquisitely cultured beau monde. You have your parallax wrong, dear lady. That upper-class milieu – the fashionable set, if you will – to which Katya belonged, had backward tastes, to put it mildly. Chekhov was considered an 'impressionist,' the society rhymster Grand Duke Constantine a major poet, and the arch-Christian Alexander Blok a wicked Jew who wrote futuristic sonnets about dying swans and lilac liqueurs. Handwritten copies of album verse, French and English, made the rounds, and were recopied in turn, not without distortions, while the author's name imperceptibly vanished, so that those outpourings quite accidentally assumed a glamorous anonymity; and, generally speaking, it is amusing to juxtapose their meanderings with the clandestine copying of seditious jingles practiced in lower circles. A good indication of how undeservedly these male and female monologues about love were considered most modern examples of foreign lyricism is the fact that the darling among them was a piece by poor Louis Bouilhet, who wrote in the middle of the last century. Reveling in the rolling cadences, Katya would declaim his alexandrines, and scold me for finding fault with a certain highly sonorous strophe in which, after having referred to his passion as a violin bow, the author compares his mistress to a guitar.

Apropos of guitars, Madam, you write that 'in

the evening the young people would gather and Olga would sit at a table and sing in a rich contralto.' Oh, well – one more death, one more victim of your sumptuous prose. Yet how I cherished the echoes of modish *tziganshchina* that inclined Katya to singing, and me to composing verse! Well do I know that this was no longer authentic Gypsy art such as that which enchanted Pushkin and, later, Apollon Grigoriev, but a barely breathing, jaded, and doomed muse; everything contributed to her ruin: the gramophone, the war, and various so-called *tzigane* songs. It was for good reason that Blok, in one of his customary spells of providence, wrote down whatever words he remembered from Gypsy lyrics, as if hastening to save at least this before it was too late.

Should I tell you what those husky murmurs and plaints meant to us? Should I reveal to you the image of a distant, strange world where:

> *Pendulous willow boughs slumber*
> *Drooping low over the pond,*

where, deep in the lilac bushes,

> *The nightingale sobs out her passion,*

and where all the senses are dominated by the memory of lost love, that wicked ruler of pseudo-Gypsy romanticism? Katya and I also would have liked to reminisce, but, since we had nothing yet to reminisce about, we would counterfeit the remoteness of time and push back into it our immediate happiness. We transformed everything we saw into monuments to our still nonexistent past by trying to look at a garden path, at the moon, at the weeping willows, with the same eyes with which *now* – when fully conscious of irreparable losses – we might have looked at that old, waterlogged raft on the pond, at that moon above the black cow shed. I even suppose that, thanks to a vague inspiration, we were preparing in advance for certain things, training ourselves to remember, imagining a distant past and practicing nostalgia, so that subsequently, when that past really existed for us, we would know how to cope with it, and not perish under its burden.

But what do you care about all this? When you describe my summer sojourn at the ancestral estate you dub 'Glinskoye,' you chase me into the woods and there compel me to write verse 'redolent of youth and faith in life.' This was all not quite so. While the others played tennis (using a single red ball and some Doherty racquets, heavy and saggy, found in the attic) or croquet on a ridiculously overgrown lawn with a dandelion in front of every hoop, Katya and I would make for the kitchen garden, and, squatting there, gorge ourselves on two species of strawberry – the bright-crimson 'Victoria' (*sadovaya zemlyanika*) and the Russian hautbois (*klubnika*), purplish berries often slimed by frogs; and there was also our favorite 'Ananas' variety, unripe-looking, yet wonderfully sweet. Without straightening our backs, we moved, grunting, along the furrows, and the tendons behind our knees ached, and our insides filled with a rubious weight. The hot sun bore down, and that sun, and the strawberries, and Katya's frock of tussore silk with darkening blotches under the arms, and the patina of tan on the back of her neck – all of it blended into a sense of oppressive delight; and what bliss it was, without rising, still picking berries, to clasp Katya's warm shoulder and hear her soft laughter and little grunts of greed and the crunch of her joints as she rummaged under the leaves. Forgive me if I pass directly from that orchard, floating by with the blinding gleam of its hothouses and the swaying of hairy poppies along its avenues, to the water closet where, in the pose of Rodin's *Thinker*, my head still hot from the sun, I composed my verse. It was dismal in all senses of the word, that verse; it contained the trills of nightingales from *tzigane* songs and bits of Blok, and helpless echoes of Verlaine: *Souvenir, Souvenir, que me veux-tu? L'automne* . . . – even though autumn was still far off, and my happiness shouted with its marvelous voice nearby, probably over there, by the bowling alley, behind the old lilac bushes under which lay piles of kitchen refuse, and hens walked about. In the evenings, on the veranda, the gramophone's gaping mouth, as red as the lining of a Russian general's coat, would pour forth uncontrollable Gypsy passion; or, to the tune of 'Under a Cloud the Moon's Hidden,' a menacing voice would mimic the Kaiser: 'Give me a nib and a holder, to write ultimatums it's time.' And on the garden terrace a game of *Gorodki* (townlets) was going on: Katya's father, his collar unbuttoned, one foot advanced in its soft house boot, would take aim with a cudgel as if he were firing a rifle and then hurl it with force (but wide of the mark) at the 'townlet' of skittles while the setting sun, with the tip of its final ray, brushed across the palisade of pine trunks, leaving on each a fiery band. And when night finally fell, and the house was asleep, Katya and I would look at the dark house from the park where we kept huddled on a hard, cold, invisible bench until our bones ached, and it all seemed to us like something that had already once happened long ago: the outline of the house against the pale-green sky, the sleepy movements of the foliage, our prolonged, blind kisses.

In your elegant description, with profuse dots, of that summer, you naturally do not forget for a minute – as we used to forget – that since February of that year the nation was 'under the rule of the Provisional Government,' and you oblige Katya and me to follow revolutionary events with keen concern, that is, to conduct (for dozens of pages) political and mystical conversations that – I assure you – we never had. In the first place, I would have been embarrassed to speak, with the righteous pathos you lend me, of Russia's destiny and, in the second place, Katya and I were too absorbed in each other to pay much attention to the Revolution. I need but say that my most vivid impression in that respect was a mere trifle: one day, on Million Street in St. Petersburg, a truck packed with jolly rioters made a clumsy but accurate swerve so as to deliberately squash a passing cat, which remained lying there, as a perfectly flat, neatly ironed, black rag (only the tail still belonged to a cat – it stood upright, and the tip, I think, still moved). At the time this struck me with some deep occult meaning, but I have since had occasion to see a bus, in a bucolic Spanish village, flatten by exactly the same method an exactly similar cat, so I have become disenchanted with hidden meanings. You, on the other hand, have not only exaggerated my poetic talent beyond recognition, but have made me a prophet besides, for only a prophet could have talked, in the fall of 1917, about the green pulp of Lenin's deceased brain, or the 'inner' emigration of intellectuals in Soviet Russia.

No, that fall and that winter we talked of other matters. I was in anguish. The most awful things were happening to our romance. You give a simple explanation: 'Olga began to understand that she was sensual rather than passionate, while for

Leonid it was the opposite. Their risky caresses understandably inebriated her, but deep inside there always remained a little unmelted piece' – and so on, in the same vulgar, pretentious spirit. What do you understand of our love? So far, I have deliberately avoided direct discussion of it; but now, if I were not afraid of contagion by your style, I would describe in greater detail both its fire and its underlying melancholy. Yes, there was the summer, and the foliage's omnipresent rustle, and the headlong pedaling along all of the park's winding paths, to see who would be the first to race from different directions to the *rond-point*, where the red sand was covered by the writhing serpentine tracks of our rock-hard tires, and each live, everyday detail of that final Russian summer screamed at us in desperation, 'I am real! I am now!' As long as all of this sunny euphoria managed to stay on the surface, the innate sadness of our love went no further than the devotion to a nonexistent past. But when Katya and I once again found ourselves in Petersburg, and it had already snowed more than once, and the wooden paving blocks were already filmed with that yellowish layer – a mixture of snow and horse dung – without which I cannot picture a Russian city, the flaw emerged, and we were left with nothing but torment.

I can see her now, in her black sealskin coat, with a big, flat muff and gray fur-trimmed boots, walking on her slender legs, as if on stilts, along a very slippery sidewalk; or in a dark, high-necked dress, sitting on a blue divan, her face heavily powdered after much crying. As I walked to her house in the evenings and returned after midnight, I would recognize amid the granite night, under a frosty sky, dove-gray with starlight, the imperturbable and immutable landmarks of my itinerary – always those same huge Petersburg objects, lone edifices of legendary times, adorning the nocturnal wastes and half-turning away from the traveler as all beauty does: it sees you not, it is pensive, and listless, its mind is elsewhere. I would talk to myself, exhorting fate, Katya, the stars, the columns of a huge, mute, abstracted cathedral; and when a desultory exchange of fire began in the dark streets, it would occur to me casually, and not without a sense of pleasure, that I might be picked off by a stray bullet and die right there, reclining on dim snow, in my elegant fur coat, my bowler askew, among scattered white paperbacks of Gumilyov's or Mandelshtam's new collections of verse that I had dropped and that were barely visible against the snow. Or else, sobbing and moaning as I walked, I would try to persuade myself that it was I who had stopped loving Katya, as I hastened to gather up all I could recall of her mendacity, her presumption, her vacuity, the pretty patch masking a pimple, the artificial *grasseyement* that would appear in her speech when she needlessly switched to French, her invulnerable weakness for titled poetasters, and the ill-tempered, dull expression of her eyes when, for the hundredth time, I tried to make her tell me with whom she had spent the previous evening. And when it was all gathered and weighed in the balance, I would perceive with anguish that my love, burdened as it was with all that trash, had settled and lodged only deeper, and that not even draft horses with iron muscles could haul it out of the morass. And the following evening again, I would make my way through the sailor-manned identity checks on the street corners (documents were demanded that allowed me access at least to the threshold of Katya's soul, and were invalid beyond that point); I would once again go to gaze at Katya, who, at the first pitiful word of mine, would turn into a large, rigid doll who would lower her convex eyelids and respond in china-doll language. When, one memorable night, I demanded that she give me a final, super-truthful reply, Katya simply said nothing, and, instead, remained lying motionless on the couch, her mirrorlike eyes reflecting the flame of the candle which on that night of historical turbulence substituted for electric light, and, after hearing her silence through to the end, I got up and left. Three days later, I had my valet take a note to her, in which I wrote that I would commit suicide if I could not see her just once more. So one glorious morning, with a rosy round sun and creaking snow, we met on Post Office Street; I silently kissed her hand, and for a quarter of an hour, without a single word interrupting our silence, we strolled to and fro, while nearby, on the corner of the Horse Guards Boulevard, stood smoking, with feigned nonchalance, a perfectly respectable-looking man in an astrakhan cap. As she and I silently walked to and fro, a little boy passed, pulling by its string a baized hand sled with a tattered fringe, and a drainpipe suddenly gave a rattle and disgorged a chunk of ice, while the man on the corner kept smoking; then, at precisely the same spot where we had met, I just as silently kissed her hand, which slipped back into its muff forever.

> *Farewell, my anguish and my ardor,*
> *Farewell, my dream, farewell, my pain!*
> *Along the paths of the old garden*
> *We two shall never pass again.*

Yes, yes: farewell, as the *tzigane* song has it. In spite of everything you were beautiful, impenetrably beautiful, and so adorable that I could cry, ignoring your myopic soul, and the triviality of your opinions, and a thousand minor betrayals; while I, with my overambitious verse, the heavy and hazy array of my feelings, and my breathless, stuttering speech, in spite of all my love for you, must have been contemptible and repulsive. And there is no need for me to tell you what torments I went through afterwards, how I looked and looked at the snapshot in which, with a gleam on your lip and a glint in your hair, you are looking past me. Katya, why have you made such a mess of it now?

Come, let us have a calm, heart-to-heart talk. With a lugubrious hiss the air has now been let out of the arrogant rubber fatman who, tightly inflated, clowned around at the beginning of this letter; and you, my dear, are really not a corpulent lady novelist in her novelistic hammock but the same old Katya, with Katya's calculated dash of demeanor, Katya of the narrow shoulders, a comely, discreetly made-up lady who, out of silly coquetry, has concocted a worthless book. To think that you did not even spare our parting! Leonid's letter, in which he threatens to shoot Olga, and which she discusses with her future husband; that future husband, in the role of undercover agent, standing on a street corner, ready to rush to the rescue if Leonid should draw the revolver that he is clutching in his coat pocket, as he passionately entreats Olga not to go, and keeps interrupting with his sobs her level-headed words: what a disgusting, senseless fabrication! And at the end of the book you have me join the White Army and get caught by the Reds during a reconnaissance, and, with the names of two traitresses – Russia, Olga – on my lips, die valiantly, felled by the bullet of a 'Hebrew-dark' commissar. How intensely I must have loved you if I still see you as you were sixteen years ago, make agonizing efforts to free our past from its humiliating captivity, and save your image from the rack and disgrace of your own pen! I honestly do not know, though, if I am succeeding. My letter smacks strangely of those rhymed epistles that you would rattle off by heart – remember?

The sight of my handwriting may surprise you

– but I shall refrain from closing, as Apukhtin does, with the invitation:

The sea awaits you here, as vast as love
And love, vast as the sea!

– I shall refrain, because, in the first place, there is no sea here, and, in the second, I have not the least desire to see you. For, after your book, Katya, I am afraid of you. Truly there was no point in rejoicing and suffering as we rejoiced and suffered only to find one's past besmirched in a lady's novel. Listen – stop writing books! At least let this flop serve as a lesson. 'At least,' for I have the right to wish that you will be stunned by horror upon realizing what you have perpetrated. And do you know what else I long for? Perhaps, perhaps (this is a very small and sickly 'perhaps,' but I grasp at it and hence do not sign this letter) – perhaps, after all, Katya, in spite of everything, a rare coincidence has occurred, and it is not you that wrote that tripe, and your equivocal but enchanting image has not been mutilated. In that case, please forgive me, colleague Solntsev.

Razor

His regimental comrades had good reason to dub him 'Razor.' The man's face lacked a façade. When his acquaintances thought of him they could imagine him only in profile, and that profile was remarkable: nose sharp as a draftsman's triangle; chin sturdy as an elbow; long, soft eyelashes characteristic of certain very obstinate, very cruel people. His name was Ivanov.

That nickname of former days contained a strange clairvoyance. It is not rare for a man called Stone or Stein to become a perfectly good mineralogist. Captain Ivanov, after an epic escape and sundry insipid ordeals, had ended up in Berlin, and chosen the very trade at which his nickname had hinted – that of a barber.

He worked in a small but clean barbershop that also employed two young professionals, who treated 'the Russian captain' with jovial respect. Then there was the owner, a dour lump of a man who would spin the handle of the cash register with a silvery sound, and also a manicurist, anemic and translucent as if she had been drained dry by the contact of innumerable fingers placed, in batches of five, on the small velvet cushion in front of her.

Ivanov was very good at his work, although he was somewhat handicapped by his poor knowledge of German. However, he soon figured out how to deal with the problem: tack a *'nicht'* onto the first sentence, an interrogative *'was?'* onto the next, then *'nicht'* again, continuing to alternate in the same way. And even though it was only in Berlin that he had learned haircutting, it was remarkable how closely his manner resembled that of the tonsors back in Russia, with their well-known penchant for a lot of superfluous scissor-clicking – they'll click away, take aim, and snip a lock or two, then keep their blades going lickety-split in the air as if impelled by inertia. This deft, gratuitous whirring was the very thing that earned him the respect of his colleagues.

Without doubt scissors and razors are weapons, and there was something about this metallic chirr that gratified Ivanov's warlike soul. He was a rancorous, keen-witted man. His vast, noble, splendid homeland had been ruined by some dull buffoon for the sake of a well-turned scarlet phrase, and this he could not forgive. Like a tightly coiled spring, vengeance lurked, biding its time, within his soul.

One very hot, bluish summer morning, taking advantage of the nearly total absence of customers during those workaday hours, both of Ivanov's colleagues took an hour off. Their employer, dying from the heat and from long-ripening desire, had silently escorted the pale, unresisting little manicurist to a back room. Left alone in the sun-drenched shop, Ivanov glanced through one newspaper, then lit a cigarette and, all in white, stepped outside the doorway and started watching the passersby.

People flashed past, accompanied by their blue shadows, which broke over the edge of the sidewalk and glided fearlessly underneath the glittering wheels of cars that left ribbonlike imprints on the heat-softened asphalt, resembling the ornate lacework of snakes. Suddenly a short, thickset gentleman in black suit and bowler, with a black briefcase under his arm, turned off the sidewalk and headed straight for white Ivanov. Blinking from the sun, Ivanov stepped aside to let him into the barbershop.

The newcomer's reflection appeared in all the mirrors at once: in profile, three-quarter-face, and showing the waxen bald spot in back from which the black bowler had ascended to snag a hat hook. And when the man turned squarely toward the mirrors, which sparkled above marble surfaces aglitter with green and gold scent bottles, Ivanov instantly recognized that mobile, puffy face with the piercing little eyes and a plump mole by the right lobe of his nose.

The gentleman silently sat down in front of the mirror, then, mumbling indistinctly, tapped his untidy cheek with a stubby finger: Meaning, I want a shave. In a kind of astonished haze, Ivanov spread a sheet over him, whipped up some tepid lather in a porcelain bowl, started brushing it on to the man's cheeks, rounded chin, and upper lip, gingerly circumnavigated the mole, began rubbing in the foam with his index finger. But he did all this mechanically, so shaken was he by having encountered this person again.

Now a flimsy white mask of soap covered the man's face up to his eyes, minuscule eyes that glittered like the tiny wheels of a watch movement. Ivanov had opened his razor and begun to sharpen it on a strap when he recovered from his amazement and realized that this man was in his power.

Then, bending over the waxy bald spot, he brought the blue blade close to the soapy mask and said very softly, 'My respects to you, comrade. How long has it been since you left our part of the world? No, don't move, please, or I might cut you prematurely.'

The glittering little wheels started moving faster, glanced at Ivanov's sharp profile, and stopped. Ivanov removed some excess flakes of lather with the blunt side of the razor and continued, 'I remember you very well, comrade. Sorry if I find it distasteful to pronounce your name. I remember how you interrogated me some six years ago, in Kharkov. I remember your signature, dear friend. . . . But, as you see, I am still alive.'

Then the following happened. The little eyes darted about, then suddenly shut tight, eyelids compressed like those of the savage who thought closing his eyes made him invisible.

Ivanov tenderly moved his blade along the cold, rustling cheek.

'We're absolutely alone, comrade. Understand? One little slip of the razor, and right away there will be a good deal of blood. Here is where the carotid throbs. So there will be a good deal, even a great deal of blood. But first I want your face decently shaved, and, besides, I have something to recount to you.'

Cautiously, with two fingers, Ivanov lifted the fleshy tip of the man's nose and, with the same tenderness, began shaving above the upper lip.

'The point, comrade, is that I remember everything. I remember perfectly, and I want you to remember too. . . .' And, in a soft voice, Ivanov began his account, as he unhurriedly shaved the recumbent, motionless face. The tale he told must have been terrifying indeed, because from time to time his hand would stop, and he would stoop very close to the gentleman sitting like a corpse under the shroudlike sheet, his convex eyelids lowered.

'That is all,' Ivanov said with a sigh, 'that's the whole story. Tell me, what do you think would be a suitable atonement for all that? What is considered an equivalent of a sharp sword? And again, keep in mind that we are utterly, totally alone.

'Corpses are always shaved,' went on Ivanov, running the blade upward along the stretched skin of the man's neck. 'Those sentenced to death are shaved too. And now I am shaving you. Do you realize what is going to happen next?'

The man sat without stirring or opening his eyes. Now the lathery mask was gone from his face. Traces of foam remained only on his cheek-bones and near his ears. This tensed, eyeless, fat face was so pallid that Ivanov wondered if he had not suffered a fit of paralysis. But when he pressed the flat surface of the razor to the man's neck, his entire body gave a twitch. He did not, however, open his eyes.

Ivanov gave the man's face a quick wipe and spat some talcum on him from a pneumatic dispenser. 'That will do for you,' he said. 'I'm satis-fied. You may leave.' With squeamish haste he yanked the sheet off the man's shoulders. The other remained seated.

'Get up, you ninny,' shouted Ivanov, pulling him up by the sleeve. The man froze, with firmly shut eyes, in the middle of the shop. Ivanov clapped the bowler on his head, thrust the briefcase under his arm, and swiveled him toward the door. Only then did the man jerk into motion. His shut-eyed face flashed in all the mirrors. He stepped like an automaton through the door that Ivanov was holding open, and, with the same mechanical gait, clutching his briefcase with an outstretched petrified hand, gazing into the sunny blur of the street with the glazed eyes of a Greek statue, he was gone.

A Russian Beauty

Olga, of whom we are about to speak, was born in the year 1900, in a wealthy, carefree family of nobles. A pale little girl in a white sailor suit, with a side parting in her chestnut hair and such merry eyes that everyone kissed her there, she was deemed a beauty since childhood. The purity of her profile, the expression of her closed lips, the silkiness of her tresses that reached to the small of her back – all this was enchanting indeed.

Her childhood passed festively, securely, and gaily, as was the custom in our country since the days of old. A sunbeam falling on the cover of a *Bibliothèque Rose* volume at the family estate, the classical hoarfrost of the Saint Petersburg public gardens. . . . A supply of memories, such as these, comprised her sole dowry when she left Russia in the spring of 1919. Everything happened in full accord with the style of the period. Her mother died of typhus, her brother was executed by the firing squad. All these are ready-made formulae, of course, the usual dreary small talk, but it all did happen, there is no other way of saying it, and it's no use turning up your nose.

Well, then, in 1919 we have a grown-up young

lady, with a pale, broad face that overdid things in terms of the regularity of its features, but just the same very lovely. Tall, with soft breasts, she always wears a black jumper and a scarf around her white neck and holds an English cigarette in her slender-fingered hand with a prominent little bone just above the wrist.

Yet there was a time in her life, at the end of 1916 or so, when at a summer resort near the family estate there was no schoolboy who did not plan to shoot himself because of her, there was no university student who would not . . . In a word, there had been a special magic about her, which, had it lasted, would have caused . . . would have wreaked . . . But somehow, nothing came of it. Things failed to develop, or else happened to no purpose. There were flowers that she was too lazy to put in a vase, there were strolls in the twilight now with this one, now with another, followed by the blind alley of a kiss.

She spoke French fluently, pronouncing *les gens* (the servants) as if rhyming with *agence* and splitting *août* (August) in two syllables (*a-ou*). She naively translated the Russian *grabezhi* (robberies) as *les grabuges* (quarrels) and used some archaic French locutions that had somehow survived in old Russian families, but she rolled her *r*'s most convincingly even though she had never been to France. Over the dresser in her Berlin room a postcard of Serov's portrait of the Tsar was fastened with a pin with a fake turquoise head. She was religious, but at times a fit of giggles would overcome her in church. She wrote verse with that terrifying facility typical of young Russian girls of her generation: patriotic verse, humorous verse, any kind of verse at all.

For about six years, that is until 1926, she resided in a boarding-house on the Augsburgerstrasse (not far from the clock), together with her father, a broad-shouldered, beetle-browed old man with a yellowish mustache, and with tight, narrow trousers on his spindly legs. He had a job with some optimistic firm, was noted for his decency and kindness, and was never one to turn down a drink.

In Berlin, Olga gradually acquired a large group of friends, all of them young Russians. A certain jaunty tone was established. 'Let's go to the cinemonkey,' or 'That was a heely deely German *Diele*, dance hall.' All sorts of popular sayings, cant phrases, imitations of imitations were much in demand. 'These cutlets are grim.' 'I wonder who's kissing her now?' Or, in a hoarse, choking voice: '*Mes-sieurs les officiers . . .*'

At the Zotovs', in their overheated rooms, she languidly danced the fox-trot to the sound of the gramophone, shifting the elongated calf of her leg not without grace and holding away from her the cigarette she had just finished smoking, and when her eyes located the ashtray that revolved with the music she would shove the butt into it, without missing a step. How charmingly, how meaningfully she could raise the wineglass to her lips, secretly drinking to the health of a third party as she looked through her lashes at the one who had confided in her. How she loved to sit in the corner of the sofa, discussing with this person or that somebody else's affairs of the heart, the oscillation of chances, the probability of a declaration – all this indirectly, by hints – and how understandingly her eyes would smile, pure, wide-open eyes with barely noticeable freckles on the thin, faintly bluish skin underneath and around them. But as for herself, no one fell in love with her, and this was why she long remembered the boor who pawed her at a charity ball and afterwards wept on her bare shoulder. He was challenged to a duel by the little Baron R., but refused to fight. The word 'boor,' by the way, was used by Olga on any and every occasion. 'Such boors,' she would sing out in chest tones, languidly and affectionately. 'What a boor . . .' 'Aren't they boors?'

But presently her life darkened. Something was finished, people were already getting up to leave. How quickly! Her father died, she moved to another street. She stopped seeing her friends, knitted the little bonnets in fashion, and gave cheap French lessons at some ladies' club or other. In this way her life dragged on to the age of thirty.

She was still the same beauty, with that enchanting slant of the widely spaced eyes and with that rarest line of lips into which the geometry of the smile seems to be already inscribed. But her hair lost its shine and was poorly cut. Her black tailored suit was in its fourth year. Her hands, with their glistening but untidy fingernails, were roped with veins and were shaking from nervousness and from her wretched continuous smoking. And we'd best pass over in silence the state of her stockings. . . .

Now, when the silken insides of her handbag were in tatters (at least there was always the hope of finding a stray coin); now, when she was so tired; now, when putting on her only pair of shoes she had to force herself not to think of their soles, just as when, swallowing her pride, she entered the tobacconist's, she forbade herself to think of how much she already owed there; now that there was no longer the least hope of returning to Russia, and hatred had become so habitual that it almost ceased to be a sin; now that the sun was getting behind the chimney, Olga would occasionally be tormented by the luxury of certain advertisements, written in the saliva of Tantalus, imagining herself wealthy, wearing that dress, sketched with the aid of three or four insolent lines, on that ship-deck, under that palm tree, at the balustrade of that white terrace. And then there was also another thing or two that she missed.

One day, almost knocking her off her feet, her one-time friend Vera rushed like a whirlwind out of a telephone booth, in a hurry as always, loaded with parcels, with a shaggy-eyed terrier whose leash immediately became wound twice around her skirt. She pounced upon Olga, imploring her to come and stay at their summer villa, saying that it was fate itself, that it was wonderful and how have you been and are there many suitors. 'No, my dear, I'm no longer that age,' answered Olga, 'and besides. . . .' She added a little detail and Vera burst out laughing, letting her parcels sink almost to the ground. 'No, seriously,' said Olga, with a smile. Vera continued coaxing her, pulling at the terrier, turning this way and that. Olga, starting all at once to speak through her nose, borrowed some money from her.

Vera adored arranging things, be it a party with punch, a visa, or a wedding. Now she avidly took up arranging Olga's fate. 'The matchmaker within you has been aroused,' joked her husband, an elderly Balt (shaven head, monocle). Olga arrived on a bright August day. She was immediately dressed in one of Vera's frocks, her hairdo and make-up were changed. She swore languidly, but yielded, and how festively the floorboards creaked in the merry little villa! How the little mirrors, suspended in the green orchard to frighten off birds, flashed and sparkled!

A Russified German named Forstmann, a well-off athletic widower, author of books on hunting, came to spend a week. He had long been asking

Vera to find him a bride, 'a real Russian beauty.'
He had a massive, strong nose with a fine pink vein
on its high bridge. He was polite, silent, at times
even morose, but knew how to form, instantly and
while no one noticed, an eternal friendship with a
dog or with a child. With his arrival Olga became
difficult. Listless and irritable, she did all the wrong
things and she knew that they were wrong. When
the conversation turned to old Russia (Vera tried
to make her show off her past), it seemed to her
that everything she said was a lie and that everyone
understood that it was a lie, and therefore she stubbornly refused to say the things that Vera was
trying to extract from her and in general would
not cooperate in any way.

On the veranda, they would slam their cards
down hard. Everyone would go off together for a
stroll through the woods, but Forstmann conversed
mostly with Vera's husband, and, recalling some
pranks of their youth, the two of them would turn
red with laughter, lag behind, and collapse on the
moss. On the eve of Forstmann's departure they
were playing cards on the veranda, as they usually
did in the evening. Suddenly, Olga felt an impossible spasm in her throat. She still managed to smile
and to leave without undue haste. Vera knocked
on her door but she did not open. In the middle
of the night, having swatted a multitude of sleepy
flies and smoked continuously to the point where
she was no longer able to inhale, irritated,

depressed, hating herself and everyone, Olga went into the garden. There, the crickets stridulated, the branches swayed, an occasional apple fell with a taut thud, and the moon performed calisthenics on the whitewashed wall of the chicken coop.

Early in the morning, she came out again and sat down on the porch step that was already hot. Forstmann, wearing a dark blue bathrobe, sat next to her and, clearing his throat, asked if she would consent to become his spouse – that was the very word he used: 'spouse.' When they came to breakfast, Vera, her husband, and his maiden cousin, in utter silence, were performing nonexistent dances, each in a different corner, and Olga drawled out in an affectionate voice 'What boors!' and next summer she died in childbirth.

That's all. Of course, there may be some sort of sequel, but it is not known to me. In such cases, instead of getting bogged down in guesswork, I repeat the words of the merry king in my favorite fairy tale: Which arrow flies forever? The arrow that has hit its mark.

Cloud, Castle, Lake

One of my representatives – a modest, mild bachelor, very efficient – happened to win a pleasure trip at a charity ball given by Russian refugees. That was in 1936 or 1937. The Berlin summer was in full flood (it was the second week of damp and cold, so that it was a pity to look at everything which had turned green in vain, and only the sparrows kept cheerful); he did not care to go anywhere, but when he tried to sell his ticket at the office of the Bureau of Pleasantrips he was told that to do so he would have to have special permission from the Ministry of Transportation; when he tried them, it turned out that first he would have to draw up a complicated petition at a notary's on stamped paper; and besides, a so-called 'certificate of nonabsence from the city for the summertime' had to be obtained from the police.

So he sighed a little, and decided to go. He borrowed an aluminum flask from friends, repaired his soles, bought a belt and a fancy-style flannel shirt – one of those cowardly things which shrink in the first wash. Incidentally, it was too large for that likable little man, his hair always neatly trimmed, his eyes so intelligent and kind. I cannot

34

remember his name at the moment. I think it was Vasiliy Ivanovich.

He slept badly the night before the departure. And why? Because he had to get up unusually early, and hence took along into his dreams the delicate face of the watch ticking on his night table; but mainly because that very night, for no reason at all, he began to imagine that this trip, thrust upon him by a feminine fate in a low-cut gown, this trip which he had accepted so reluctantly, would bring him some wonderful, tremulous happiness. This happiness would have something in common with his childhood, and with the excitement aroused in him by Russian lyrical poetry, and with some evening skyline once seen in a dream, and with that lady, another man's wife, whom he had hopelessly loved for seven years – but it would be even fuller and more significant than all that. And besides, he felt that the really good life must be oriented toward something or someone.

The morning was dull, but steam-warm and close, with an inner sun, and it was quite pleasant to rattle in a streetcar to the distant railway station where the gathering place was: several people, alas, were taking part in the excursion. Who would they be, these drowsy beings, drowsy as seem all creatures still unknown to us? By Window Number 6, at seven a.m., as was indicated in the directions appended to the ticket, he saw them (they were already waiting; he had managed to be late by about three minutes).

A lanky blond young man in Tyrolese garb stood out at once. He was burned the color of a cockscomb, had huge brick-red knees with golden hairs, and his nose looked lacquered. He was the leader furnished by the Bureau, and as soon as the newcomer had joined the group (which consisted of four women and as many men) he led it off toward a train lurking behind other trains, carrying his monstrous knapsack with terrifying ease, and firmly clanking with his hobnailed boots.

Everyone found a place in an empty car, unmistakably third-class, and Vasiliy Ivanovich, having sat down by himself and put a peppermint into his mouth, opened a little volume of Tyutchev, whom he had long intended to reread; but he was requested to put the book aside and join the group. An elderly bespectacled post-office clerk, with skull, chin, and upper lip a bristly blue as if he had shaved off some extraordinarily luxuriant and tough growth especially for this trip, immediately announced that he had been to Russia and knew some Russian – for instance, *patzlui* – and, recalling philanderings in Tsaritsyn, winked in such a manner that his fat wife sketched out in the air the outline of a backhand box on the ear. The company was getting noisy. Four employees of the same building firm were tossing each other heavy-weight jokes: a middle-aged man, Schultz; a younger man,

Schultz also, and two fidgety young women with big mouths and big rumps. The red-headed, rather burlesque widow in a sport skirt knew something too about Russia (the Riga beaches). There was also a dark young man by the name of Schramm, with lusterless eyes and a vague velvety vileness about his person and manners, who constantly switched the conversation to this or that attractive aspect of the excursion, and who gave the first signal for rapturous appreciation; he was, as it turned out later, a special stimulator from the Bureau of Pleasantrips.

The locomotive, working rapidly with its elbows, hurried through a pine forest, then – with relief – among fields. Only dimly realizing as yet all the absurdity and horror of the situation, and perhaps attempting to persuade himself that everything was very nice, Vasiliy Ivanovich contrived to enjoy the fleeting gifts of the road. And indeed, how enticing it all is, what charm the world acquires when it is wound up and moving like a merry-go-round! The sun crept toward a corner of the window and suddenly spilled over the yellow bench. The badly pressed shadow of the car sped madly along the grassy bank, where flowers blended into colored streaks. A crossing: a cyclist was waiting, one foot resting on the ground. Trees appeared in groups and singly, revolving coolly and blandly, displaying the latest fashions. The blue dampness of a ravine. A memory of love, disguised as a meadow. Wispy clouds – greyhounds of heaven.

We both, Vasiliy Ivanovich and I, have always been impressed by the anonymity of all the parts of a landscape, so dangerous for the soul, the impossibility of ever finding out where that path you see leads – and look, what a tempting thicket! It happened that on a distant slope or in a gap in the trees there would appear and, as it were, stop for an instant, like air retained in the lungs, a spot so enchanting – a lawn, a terrace – such perfect expression of tender well-meaning beauty – that it seemed that if one could stop the train and go thither, forever, to you, my love . . . But a thousand beech trunks were already madly leaping by, whirling in a sizzling sun pool, and again the chance for happiness was gone.

At the stations, Vasiliy Ivanovich would look at the configuration of some entirely insignificant objects – a smear on the platform, a cherry stone, a cigarette butt – and would say to himself that never, never would he remember these three little things here in that particular interrelation, this pattern, which he now could see with such deathless precision; or again, looking at a group of children waiting for a train, he would try with all his might to single out at least one remarkable destiny – in the form of a violin or a crown, a propeller or a lyre – and would gaze until the whole party of village schoolboys appeared as in an old photograph, now reproduced with a little white cross above the face of the last boy on the right: the hero's childhood.

But one could look out of the window only by snatches. All had been given sheet music with verses from the Bureau:

> *Stop that worrying and moping,*
> *Take a knotted stick and rise,*
> *Come a-tramping in the open*
> *With the good, the hearty guys!*

> *Tramp your country's grass and stubble,*
> *With the good, the hearty guys,*
> *Kill the hermit and his trouble*
> *And to hell with doubts and sighs!*

> *In a paradise of heather*
> *Where the field mouse screams and dies,*
> *Let us march and sweat together*
> *With the steel-and-leather guys!*

This was to be sung in chorus: Vasiliy Ivanovich, who not only could not sing but could not even pronounce German words clearly, took advantage of the drowning roar of mingling voices and merely opened his mouth while swaying slightly, as if he were really singing – but the leader, at a sign from the subtle Schramm, suddenly stopped the general singing and, squinting askance at

Vasiliy Ivanovich, demanded that he sing solo. Vasiliy Ivanovich cleared his throat, timidly began, and after a minute of solitary torment all joined in; but he did not dare thereafter to drop out.

He had with him his favorite cucumber from the Russian store, a loaf of bread, and three eggs. When evening came, and the low crimson sun entered wholly the soiled seasick car, stunned by its own din, all were invited to hand over their provisions, in order to divide them evenly – this was particularly easy, as all except Vasiliy Ivanovich had the same things. The cucumber amused everybody, was pronounced inedible, and was thrown out of the window. In view of the insufficiency of his contribution, Vasiliy Ivanovich got a smaller portion of sausage.

He was made to play cards. They pulled him about, questioned him, verified whether he could show the route of the trip on a map – in a word, all busied themselves with him, at first good-naturedly, then with malevolence, which grew with the approach of night. Both girls were called Greta; the red-headed widow somehow resembled the rooster-leader; Schramm, Schultz, and the other Schultz, the post-office clerk and his wife, all gradually melted together, merged together, forming one collective, wobbly, many-handed being, from which one could not escape. It pressed upon him from all sides. But suddenly at some station all climbed out, and it was already dark, although in the west there still hung a very long, very pink cloud, and farther along the track, with a soul-piercing light, the star of a lamp trembled through the slow smoke of the engine, and crickets chirped in the dark, and from somewhere there came the odor of jasmine and hay, my love.

They spent the night in a tumble-down inn. A mature bedbug is awful, but there is a certain grace in the motions of silky silverfish. The post-office clerk was separated from his wife, who was put with the widow; he was given to Vasiliy Ivanovich for the night. The two beds took up the whole room. Quilt on top, chamber pot below. The clerk said that somehow he did not feel sleepy, and began to talk of his Russian adventures, rather more circumstantially than in the train. He was a great bully of a man, thorough and obstinate, clad in long cotton drawers, with mother-of-pearl claws on his dirty toes, and bear's fur between fat breasts. A moth dashed about the ceiling, hobnobbing with its shadow. 'In Tsaritsyn,' the clerk was saying, 'there are now three schools, a German, a Czech, and a Chinese one. At any rate, that is what my brother-in-law says; he went there to build tractors.'

Next day, from early morning to five o'clock in the afternoon, they raised dust along a highway, which undulated from hill to hill; then they took a green road through a dense fir wood. Vasiliy Ivanovich, as the least burdened, was given an enormous round loaf of bread to carry under his arm. How I hate you, our daily! But still his precious, experienced eyes noted what was necessary. Against the background of fir-tree gloom a dry needle was hanging vertically on an invisible thread.

Again they piled into a train, and again the small partitionless car was empty. The other Schultz began to teach Vasiliy Ivanovich how to play the mandolin. There was much laughter. When they got tired of that, they thought up a capital game, which was supervised by Schramm. It consisted of the following: the women would lie down on the benches they chose, under which the men were already hidden, and when from under one of the benches there would emerge a ruddy face with ears, or a big outspread hand, with a skirt-lifting curve of the fingers (which would provoke much squealing), then it would be revealed who was paired off with whom. Three times Vasiliy Ivanovich lay down in filthy darkness, and three times it turned out that there was no one on the bench when he crawled out from under. He was acknowledged the loser and was forced to eat a cigarette butt.

They spent the night on straw mattresses in a barn, and early in the morning set out again on foot. Firs, ravines, foamy streams. From the heat, from the songs which one had constantly to bawl, Vasiliy Ivanovich became so exhausted that during the midday halt he fell asleep at once, and awoke only when they began to slap at imaginary horse-flies on him. But after another hour of marching, that very happiness of which he had once half dreamt was suddenly discovered.

It was a pure, blue lake, with an unusual expression of its water. In the middle, a large cloud was reflected in its entirety. On the other side, on a hill thickly covered with verdure (and the darker the verdure, the more poetic it is), towered, arising from dactyl to dactyl, an ancient black castle. Of course, there are plenty of such views in Central Europe, but just this one – in the inexpressible and unique harmoniousness of its three principal parts, in its smile, in some mysterious innocence it had, my love! my obedient one! – was something so unique, and so familiar, and so long-promised, and it so *understood* the beholder that Vasiliy Ivanovich even pressed his hand to his heart, as if to see whether his heart was there in order to give it away.

At some distance, Schramm, poking into the air with the leader's alpenstock, was calling the attention of the excursionists to something or other; they had settled themselves around on the grass in poses seen in amateur snapshots, while the leader sat on a stump, his behind to the lake, and was having a snack. Quietly, concealing himself in his own shadow, Vasiliy Ivanovich followed the shore, and came to a kind of inn. A dog still quite young greeted him; it crept on its belly, its jaws laughing, its tail fervently beating the ground.

Vasiliy Ivanovich accompanied the dog into the house, a piebald two-storied dwelling with a winking window beneath a convex tiled eyelid; and he found the owner, a tall old man vaguely resembling a Russian war veteran, who spoke German so poorly and with such a soft drawl that Vasiliy Ivanovich changed to his own tongue, but the man understood as in a dream and continued in the language of his environment, his family.

Upstairs was a room for travelers. 'You know, I shall take it for the rest of my life,' Vasiliy Ivanovich is reported to have said as soon as he had entered it. The room itself had nothing remarkable about it. On the contrary, it was a most ordinary room, with a red floor, daisies daubed on the white walls, and a small mirror half filled with the yellow infusion of the reflected flowers – but from the window one could clearly see the lake with its cloud and its castle, in a motionless and perfect correlation of happiness. Without reasoning, without considering, only entirely surrendering to an attraction the truth of which consisted in its own strength, a strength which he had never experienced before, Vasiliy Ivanovich in one radiant second realized that here in this little room with that view, beautiful to the verge of tears, life would at last be what he had always wished it to be. What exactly it would be like, what would take place here, that of course he did not know, but all around him were help, promise,

44

and consolation – so that there could not be any doubt that he must live here. In a moment he figured out how he would manage it so as not to have to return to Berlin again, how to get the few possessions that he had – books, the blue suit, her photograph. How simple it was turning out! As my representative, he was earning enough for the modest life of a refugee Russian.

'My friends,' he cried, having run down again to the meadow by the shore, 'my friends, good-bye. I shall remain for good in that house over there. We can't travel together any longer. I shall go no farther. I am not going anywhere. Good-bye!'

'How is that?' said the leader in a queer voice, after a short pause, during which the smile on the lips of Vasiliy Ivanovich slowly faded, while the people who had been sitting on the grass half rose and stared at him with stony eyes.

'But why?' he faltered. 'It is here that . . .'

'Silence!' the post-office clerk suddenly bellowed with extraordinary force. 'Come to your senses, you drunken swine!'

'Wait a moment, gentlemen,' said the leader, and, having passed his tongue over his lips, he turned to Vasiliy Ivanovich.

'You probably have been drinking,' he said quietly. 'Or have gone out of your mind. You are taking a pleasure trip with us. Tomorrow, according to the appointed itinerary – look at your ticket – we are all returning to Berlin. There can be no question of anyone – in this case you – refusing to continue this communal journey. We were singing today a certain song – try and remember what it said. That's enough now! Come, children, we are going on.'

'There will be beer at Ewald,' said Schramm in a caressing voice. 'Five hours by train. Hikes. A hunting lodge. Coal mines. Lots of interesting things.'

'I shall complain,' wailed Vasiliy Ivanovich. 'Give me back my bag. I have the right to remain where I want. Oh, but this is nothing less than an invitation to a beheading' – he told me he cried when they seized him by the arms.

'If necessary we shall carry you,' said the leader grimly, 'but that is not likely to be pleasant. I am responsible for each of you, and shall bring back each of you, alive or dead.'

Swept along a forest road as in a hideous fairy tale, squeezed, twisted, Vasiliy Ivanovich could not even turn around, and only felt how the radiance behind his back receded, fractured by trees, and then it was no longer there, and all around the dark firs fretted but could not interfere. As soon as everyone had got into the car and the train had pulled off, they began to beat him – they beat him a long time, and with a good deal of inventiveness. It occurred to them, among other things, to use a corkscrew on his palms; then on his feet. The post-office clerk, who had been to Russia, fashioned a knout out of a stick and a belt, and began to use it with devilish dexterity. Atta boy! The other men relied more on their iron heels, whereas the women were satisfied to pinch and slap. All had a wonderful time.

After returning to Berlin, he called on me, was much changed, sat down quietly, putting his hands on his knees, told his story; kept on repeating that he must resign his position, begged me to let him go, insisted that he could not continue, that he had not the strength to belong to mankind any longer. Of course, I let him go.

Signs and Symbols

For the fourth time in as many years they were confronted with the problem of what birthday present to bring a young man who was incurably deranged in his mind. He had no desires. Man-made objects were to him either hives of evil, vibrant with a malignant activity that he alone could perceive, or gross comforts for which no use could be found in his abstract world. After eliminating a number of articles that might offend him or frighten him (anything in the gadget line for instance was taboo), his parents chose a dainty and innocent trifle: a basket with ten different fruit jellies in ten little jars.

At the time of his birth they had been married already for a long time; a score of years had elapsed, and now they were quite old. Her drab gray hair was done anyhow. She wore cheap black dresses. Unlike other women of her age (such as Mrs. Sol, their next-door neighbor, whose face was all pink and mauve with paint and whose hat was a cluster of brookside flowers), she presented a naked white countenance to the fault-finding light of spring days. Her husband, who in the old country had been a fairly successful businessman, was now wholly dependent on his brother Isaac, a real American of almost forty years' standing. They seldom saw him and had nicknamed him 'the Prince.'

That Friday everything went wrong. The underground train lost its life current between two stations, and for a quarter of an hour one could hear nothing but the dutiful beating of one's heart and the rustling of newspapers. The bus they had to take next kept them waiting for ages; and when it did come, it was crammed with garrulous high school children. It was raining hard as they walked up the brown path leading to the sanatorium. There they waited again; and instead of their boy shuffling into the room as he usually did (his poor face botched with acne, ill-shaven, sullen, and confused), a nurse they knew, and did not care for, appeared at last and brightly explained that he had again attempted to take his life. He was all right, she said, but a visit might disturb him. The place was so miserably understaffed, and things got mislaid or mixed up so easily, that they decided not to leave their present in the office but to bring it to him next time they came.

She waited for her husband to open his umbrella and then took his arm. He kept clearing his throat in a special resonant way he had when he was upset. They reached the bus-stop shelter on the other side of the street and he closed his umbrella. A few feet away, under a swaying and dripping tree, a tiny half-dead unfledged bird was helplessly twitching in a puddle.

During the long ride to the subway station, she and her husband did not exchange a word; and every time she glanced at his old hand (swollen veins, brown-spotted skin), clasped and twitching upon the handle of his umbrella, she felt the mounting pressure of tears. As she looked around trying to hook her mind onto something, it gave her, kind of soft shock, a mixture of compassion and wonder, to notice that one of the passengers, a girl with dark hair and grubby red toenails, was weeping on the shoulder of an older woman. Whom did that woman resemble? She resembled Rebecca Borisovna, whose daughter had married one of the Soloveichiks – in Minsk, years ago.

The last time he had tried to do it, his method had been, in the doctor's words, a masterpiece of inventiveness; he would have succeeded, had not an envious fellow patient thought he was learning to fly – and stopped him. What he really wanted to do was to tear a hole in his world and escape.

The system of his delusions had been the subject of an elaborate paper in a scientific monthly, but long before that she and her husband had puzzled it out for themselves. 'Referential mania,' Herman Brink had called it. In these very rare cases the patient imagines that everything happening around him is a veiled reference to his personality and existence. He excludes real people from the conspiracy – because he considers himself to be so much more intelligent than other men. Phenomenal nature shadows him wherever he goes. Clouds in the staring sky transmit to one another, by means of slow signs, incredibly detailed information regarding him. His inmost thoughts are discussed at nightfall, in manual alphabet, by darkly gesticulating trees. Pebbles or stains or sun flecks form patterns representing in some awful way messages which he must intercept. Everything is a cipher and of everything he is the theme. Some of the spies are detached observers, such as glass surfaces and still pools; others, such as coats in store windows, are prejudiced witnesses, lynchers at heart; others again (running water, storms) are hysterical to the point of insanity, have a distorted opinion of him, and grotesquely misinterpret his actions. He must be always on his guard and devote every minute and module of life to the decoding of the undulation of things. The very air he exhales is indexed and filed away. If only the interest he provokes were limited to his immediate surroundings – but alas it is not! With distance the torrents of wild scandal increase in volume and volubility. The silhouettes of his blood corpuscles, magnified a million times, flit over vast plains; and still farther, great mountains of unbearable solidity and height sum up in terms of granite and groaning firs the ultimate truth of his being.

When they emerged from the thunder and foul air of the subway, the last dregs of the day were mixed with the streetlights. She wanted to buy some fish for supper, so she handed him the basket of jelly jars, telling him to go home. He walked up to the third landing and then remembered he had given her his keys earlier in the day.

In silence he sat down on the steps and in silence rose when some ten minutes later she came, heavily trudging upstairs, wanly smiling, shaking her head in deprecation of her silliness. They entered their two-room flat and he at once went to the mirror. Straining the corners of his mouth apart by means of his thumbs, with a horrible masklike grimace, he removed his new hopelessly uncomfortable dental plate and severed the long tusks of saliva connecting him to it. He read his Russian-language newspaper while she laid the table. Still reading, he ate the pale victuals that needed no teeth. She knew his moods and was also silent.

When he had gone to bed, she remained in the living room with her pack of soiled cards and her old albums. Across the narrow yard where the rain tinkled in the dark against some battered ash cans, windows were blandly alight and in one of them a black-trousered man with his bare elbows raised could be seen lying supine on an untidy bed. She pulled the blind down and examined the photographs. As a baby he looked more surprised than most babies. From a fold in the album, a German maid they had had in Leipzig and her fat-faced fiancé fell out. Minsk, the Revolution, Leipzig,

Berlin, Leipzig, a slanting housefront badly out of
focus. Four years old, in a park: moodily, shyly, with
puckered forehead, looking away from an eager
squirrel as he would from any other stranger. Aunt
Rosa, a fussy, angular, wild-eyed old lady, who had
lived in a tremulous world of bad news, bank-
ruptcies, train accidents, cancerous growths – until
the Germans put her to death, together with all
the people she had worried about. Age six – that
was when he drew wonderful birds with human
hands and feet, and suffered from insomnia like a
grown-up man. His cousin, now a famous chess
player. He again, aged about eight, already difficult to understand, afraid of the wallpaper in the
passage, afraid of a certain picture in a book which
merely showed an idyllic landscape with rocks on
a hillside and an old cart wheel hanging from the
branch of a leafless tree. Aged ten: the year they
left Europe. The shame, the pity, the humiliating
difficulties, the ugly, vicious, backward children he
was with in that special school. And then came a
time in his life, coinciding with a long convales-
cence after pneumonia, when those little phobias
of his which his parents had stubbornly regarded
as the eccentricities of a prodigiously gifted child
hardened as it were into a dense tangle of logically
interacting illusions, making him totally inacces-
sible to normal minds.

This, and much more, she accepted – for after
all living did mean accepting the loss of one joy

after another, not even joys in her case – mere possibilities of improvement. She thought of the endless waves of pain that for some reason or other she and her husband had to endure; of the invisible giants hurting her boy in some unimaginable fashion; of the incalculable amount of tenderness contained in the world; of the fate of this tenderness, which is either crushed, or wasted, or transformed into madness; of neglected children humming to themselves in unswept corners; of beautiful weeds that cannot hide from the farmer and helplessly have to watch the shadow of his simian stoop leave mangled flowers in its wake, as the monstrous darkness approaches.

It was past midnight when from the living room she heard her husband moan; and presently he staggered in, wearing over his nightgown the old overcoat with astrakhan collar which he much preferred to the nice blue bathrobe he had.

'I can't sleep,' he cried.

'Why,' she asked, 'why can't you sleep? You were so tired.'

'I can't sleep because I am dying,' he said and lay down on the couch.

'Is it your stomach? Do you want me to call Dr. Solov?'

'No doctors, no doctors,' he moaned. 'To the devil with doctors! We must get him out of there quick. Otherwise we'll be responsible. Responsible!' he repeated and hurled himself into a sitting position, both feet on the floor, thumping his forehead with his clenched fist.

'All right,' she said quietly, 'we shall bring him home tomorrow morning.'

'I would like some tea,' said her husband, and retired to the bathroom.

Bending with difficulty, she retrieved some playing cards and a photograph or two that had slipped from the couch to the floor: knave of hearts, nine of spades, ace of spades, Elsa and her bestial beau.

He returned in high spirits, saying in a loud voice: 'I have it all figured out. We will give him the bedroom. Each of us will spend part of the night near him and the other part on this couch. By turns. We will have the doctor see him at least twice a week. It does not matter what the Prince says. He won't have to say much anyway because it will come out cheaper.'

The telephone rang. It was an unusual hour for their telephone to ring. His left slipper had come off and he groped for it with his heel and toe as he stood in the middle of the room, and childishly, toothlessly, gaped at his wife. Having more English than he did, it was she who attended to calls.

'Can I speak to Charlie,' said a girl's dull little voice.

'What number you want? No. That is not the right number.'

The receiver was gently cradled. Her hand went to her old tired heart.

'It frightened me,' she said.

He smiled a quick smile and immediately resumed his excited monologue. They would fetch him as soon as it was day. Knives would have to be kept in a locked drawer. Even at his worst he presented no danger to other people.

The telephone rang a second time. The same toneless anxious young voice asked for Charlie.

'You have the incorrect number. I will tell you what you are doing: you are turning the letter *O* instead of the zero.'

They sat down to their unexpected festive midnight tea. The birthday present stood on the table. He sipped noisily; his face was flushed; every now and then he imparted a circular motion to his raised glass so as to make the sugar dissolve more thoroughly. The vein on the side of his bald head where there was a large birthmark stood out conspicuously and, although he had shaved that morning, a silvery bristle showed on his chin. While she poured him another glass of tea, he put on his spectacles and reexamined with pleasure the luminous yellow, green, red little jars. His clumsy moist lips spelled out their eloquent labels: apricot, grape, beech plum, quince. He had got to crab apple, when the telephone rang again.

POCKET PENGUINS

1. Lady Chatterley's Trial
2. **Eric Schlosser** Cogs in the Great Machine
3. **Nick Hornby** Otherwise Pandemonium
4. **Albert Camus** Summer in Algiers
5. **P. D. James** Innocent House
6. **Richard Dawkins** The View from Mount Improbable
7. **India Knight** On Shopping
8. **Marian Keyes** Nothing Bad Ever Happens in Tiffany's
9. **Jorge Luis Borges** The Mirror of Ink
10. **Roald Dahl** A Taste of the Unexpected
11. **Jonathan Safran Foer** The Unabridged Pocketbook of Lightning
12. **Homer** The Cave of the Cyclops
13. **Paul Theroux** Two Stars
14. **Elizabeth David** Of Pageants and Picnics
15. **Anaïs Nin** Artists and Models
16. **Antony Beevor** Christmas at Stalingrad
17. **Gustave Flaubert** The Desert and the Dancing Girls
18. **Anne Frank** The Secret Annexe
19. **James Kelman** Where I Was
20. **Hari Kunzru** Noise
21. **Simon Schama** The Bastille Falls
22. **William Trevor** The Dressmaker's Child
23. **George Orwell** In Defence of English Cooking
24. **Michael Moore** Idiot Nation
25. **Helen Dunmore** Rose, 1944
26. **J. K. Galbraith** The Economics of Innocent Fraud
27. **Gervase Phinn** The School Inspector Calls
28. **W. G. Sebald** Young Austerlitz
29. **Redmond O'Hanlon** Borneo and the Poet
30. **Ali Smith** Ali Smith's Supersonic 70s
31. **Sigmund Freud** Forgetting Things
32. **Simon Armitage** King Arthur in the East Riding
33. **Hunter S. Thompson** Happy Birthday, Jack Nicholson
34. **Vladimir Nabokov** Cloud, Castle, Lake
35. **Niall Ferguson** 1914: Why the World Went to War

POCKET PENGUINS